THE ANIMALS OF FARTHING WOOD

The Adventures of Mole

Colin Dann
Adapted by Clare Dannatt
Licensed by BBC Enterprises Ltd

RED FOX

Mole held tightly on to Badger's back. Behind him he could see all the animals of Farthing Wood hopping, running and crawling along.

Mole felt lucky to have his good friend to carry him, for the animals were on a long journey from their old home to the White Deer Park Nature Reserve. There, they would be safe from humans. But right now they had to cross a big stretch of marsh before bedtime.

'I'm not too heavy, am I?' Mole asked Badger anxiously.

'No – though I'm surprised, after all those worms you just ate,' teased Badger.

'Stop, everybody,' called their leader, Fox. 'We've lost Toad. I'm going back for him. You must all stay here and wait together. This is dangerous land.'

Mole slid down Badger's tail to the ground. 'Just stretching my legs,' he explained.

All the animals were lying about resting. Mole crept away quietly and began to dig a tunnel. Those worms he'd eaten at their last stop had been very tasty. He would just dig down a little way, and have one more worm.

Mole was soon deep underground, munching happily on a fat worm. Far, far above him he heard the muffled calls of his friends.

'Mole! Where are you?'

'Moley?'

'Perhaps I should go back,' thought Mole. Then he caught sight of another juicy worm's tail wriggling ahead of him.

'I'll just try this one, quickly. Then I'll go back to the others.' Mole started digging towards the tempting worm.

Mmmm! Delicious! Mole licked his lips. Maybe if he went just a little further . . . His friends weren't calling for him any more. Perhaps they were having another rest.

Splash! What was that? Mole put his paw to his head. It was wet. Splash! Mole looked up and – splash! – water fell into his eyes. Water was dripping down into his tunnel! He'd better hurry back. But when Mole started to climb up the tunnel, a wave of water soaked his fur.

'I'll just have to find another way out,' panicked Mole. He turned around and started tunnelling fast.

As Mole tunnelled on, the earth got warmer and warmer. Soon his paws were stinging from the heat. He stopped, panting for breath and wiping sweat from his forehead.

'Oh, why does everything bad always happen to me?' he wailed. 'If I go on, I'll burn, and if I go back, I'll drown. But it's all my own fault.'

Mole sat down and started to howl. 'Oh Badger, Badger, somebody, help me.'

Nobody heard Mole's cries. He wiped his eyes and sat down to think.

'I can't give up,' he told himself bravely. 'Badger wouldn't. I shall have to stay here and see what happens. And I promise, if I ever, ever get out of here I'll never be greedy again. I promise, I promise.'

Mole lay and sobbed himself to sleep.

'Thump! Thump!' Mole jumped out of his doze. What was that? 'Thump! Thump!' Human footsteps! Mole listened to the sound above him fade away.

'Perhaps the humans have stopped the water,' thought Mole. 'I could try tunnelling up again. It's getting too hot to stay here anyway.'

'It's cooler,' gasped Mole, tunnelling hard for the surface.

At last he broke free above ground. But what was that strange burning smell? Mole's nose twitched as he squinted about him in the bright daylight. All he could see was black earth and smoking grass. Where was the lovely green marsh? And where were all his friends?

'Oh Badger, oh Fox, what's happened? I'm all alone, all alone!'

Mole rested his head on his paws and wept. He was crying so hard that he did not notice the human towering above him.

Suddenly, Mole felt himself flying up through the air! Something had picked him up – he was held by a human hand! Mole screamed, but no one answered apart from the human, who stroked Mole's head with his finger. Mole trembled – he could never tell if humans were friendly or not.

Then the world turned upside down again, and Mole found himself falling down through darkness. The man had put him in his pocket!

Mole lay still for a moment. Then he started scrambling up from the bottom of the pocket. It was slippery, and much harder than climbing up a tunnel.

At last he reached the top and peered over. The ground was so far away it made Mole feel dizzy just looking. He had never been so high up in his life before. He tried to shout, but nothing came out of his mouth.

Suddenly the man started to run. Mole was jolted back inside the pocket and fell to the bottom. Then there was stillness.

Mole lay stunned for a while. Then he blinked and started to climb towards a chink of light. When he peered out of the pocket again, Mole saw more humans around, hosing a huge, blazing fire with water. So that was why his tunnel had been wet – and why it had been so hot, too.

Had the other animals escaped? Was Mole the only one left from Farthing Wood?

Mole realised he didn't have time to think any more about what had happened to his friends. Looking around him, Mole saw that the jacket he was in had been taken off by his human and left hanging on a fire engine. This was his chance of freedom!

Mole clambered out of the pocket, swung from the edge and then dropped to the ground. He sighed with relief to feel solid earth under his paws again. But where should he go? Were any of his friends left for him to find?

Mole felt very wobbly. He wandered about, hardly noticing the big human feet he was so near. The daylight and the fire were all too bright for his eyes. So little Mole did not see that his friends were very close.

Out of nowhere, Mole felt a cool snout nuzzling him. No – it couldn't be – yes! It was his friend Fox, come to rescue him.

'Quick, climb on to my tail,' whispered Fox. 'The birds are distracting the humans. But we must hurry.'

Mole clutched Fox's fiery red tail – and once again that day felt himself hurtling through space.

Fox ran with Mole through some shallow water to an island. Peeping out from Fox's bushy tail, Mole could see that all his friends were waiting for them. They had found somewhere safe to escape from the fire – which the falling rain would help to put out. And Mole wasn't lost any more.

All the animals cheered, but Mole hid his face shyly. He thought they must be cheering for Fox's bravery, not for his return.

Badger picked up Mole in both paws.

'I'm sorry,' Mole blurted out. 'I promise I'll never be greedy again. And – and I don't mind if you don't want to be friends with me any more.'

'Don't be silly, Mole,' said Badger, 'I really missed you. Do you want a ride on my back?'

'I think I'll walk for a bit, thank you very much, Badger. I've had rather a lot of rides today, for a mole.'